Niceties:
Aural Ardor, Pardon Me

Elizabeth Mikesch

Niceties

Aural Ardor, Pardon Me

ISBN (13): 978-0-9831633-9-8

art & design by Cal A. Mari

published by Calamari Press

New York, NY

< www.calamaripress.com >

Server Dance

Harshities

Siblant Bling

for the meanness in the nicest

Server Dance

When We Were French

Would we say that we would go a ways to the place of the one who we could never name? These days, where we slumber under shitshingled roofs, stuck in the crooks of our husbands, we are not yet asleep inside the bungalows dreaming of him.

It was on the floor, a spill of us, or where we wanted to lead him to weep with us, how we would do odes to him—lie down on the varnish, hand to knob, to feel holiest, close, up to the notes.

It was like this when we were still called after him.

This is how we talk about it now.

Put him down like a race dog, say, where the game was, say what we looked at, but what we saw was the slouching over of a junior leaning on his dungarees, and we dribbled, we drooled at his crooning. Oh, to jump at jeaned knees!

Boils, goiters, a burn—such an ugly thing it is to bear. He wished us toward a hand we hoped would head toward what to worship when he croaked his froggy croon from his armchair. So long as there is another dance to dance, we wanted to etch the lines of the songs we sung on top of armoires, inside our legs, so he would begin to love them with us.

We are antiques, we could say.

We learned to listen for tires out bay windows on the gravel. We never teach them, never tell them, our girls, but they follow. They wait for the tires, too.

It would please us to be asked our opinions.

(Oh, the lacquer of gymnasiums).

It was the nameless earliness that cost, a stench in the fields that gave out in long winds, that made us hate to take turns looking for his looking at one of us. It was every day we did this. Did he hear how we followed? We thought he was watching out the window. Did he know, we mean? There were others, too, who we lost.

Would we say how a light lit that was not yet the new gray dawn? That a rock, the moon, dipped down. That that man was full. When it rose, it swooned us, and we were of it. It was blooming, it was boys, their tangled legs, their sliming privates: a taste, the welt of waiting to be picked up by someone, something spoiled yellow.

It was the waiting, that dancing we tiptoed through and following, and those boys could not lead us. No. They did not yet know how to move.

There was a quickness once that we wore upon wired wrists. It hung limp, seam to waist. We crab-crawled not to trip with mixing bowls up on our heads to practice grace. We had high heels and wobbled like sea birds when we strolled.

Should you fall, should we say, fall on bended knees—should you skate. He told us this, our father, but never looked up from his news.

That joke white and red and black—what was it he would say?

A heart is a brittle thing, a taco kit on a grocery list.

There were hands to believe would make their way to your somewhere soft, to turn a person purple, to be made to feel older. Now, we wear our colors, cover lids of the leftover dishes. Our arms have floured. We sprout melanoma, lose hemoglobin. What could we tell them, but to keep their née?

Once our long hair held a waving plait, well-wound, a headached braid that was au François, halfed, split in two by a fine-toothed comb.

It ached.

Braces tugged once and cut. We wrestled out chunks of hot lunch, hid metal grins behind clipped fingernails, whispered of goings on, who with and who all did it with him over tidbits of fruit pale that swam in noontime cups. We kept plastic forks that we ought to wash.

We were sleeveless daughters once in the sleet nights of the wild fields, smokes and talk, eyelids stained, in the spunout drives, riding suicide, in the chardark, in the moonlight. There was hiding coughing—do not make a sound—inhale a puff of a poison, did the coffin slam shut? Rubbing off fingernail color, reciting "touché le table"—fingers ginger on the lacquered wood, tapping sendoffs to the ones who wore the coveralls.

What about his knocktooth kissing? How could we say?

You are too soon to forget the swelling from the cold lick of indigo light, bellies burned by mowed lawns, by the not yet sun. We wore bikinis and felt like flamingos—long-legged & lost.

You could say this: we were on a cusp.

Once we were darlings, starving for helpings—flat-butted, spank-skinned, little-hipped, pimpled. There was a film in our bottoms—a discharge, a milk. Once, they told us, we bathed in our kitchen sinks. We looked down at the wool rub dinge and did not believe them, not once, but we did do the dishes. We were sugar cookies, corsages, then whiffs of new perfumes. We got lost in them, boutonnièred, and then cologned.

Be good, Girls, he told us.

So, we tell them so, too.

Think not of dumb mothers or overripe tongues.

Conjure summer.

So, the dull wool of new school sweaters were bought for us in rough rouge, for the bleacherettes, clove smokers, snuck liquors we had become.

It is time to button up.

Do not act like you do not know.

Say, not so fast, and first use one.

A placeless wanting—no. No one finger could put on.

Damp-backed hover-overs, remember?

Splay.

Lie down.

Conjure autumn: a flourishing fog hung above, the headlight rush and bathed-in goos of ahs and night, kept lawns, the sprinklers' tongue and the sparklers' poor stars. The spilled kisses, nauseous thrum of passing class glances, the music of it wet. Our feet with painted toes, one by one on the accent rugs, a spill you cannot rub out.

You have got to listen for it.

Conjure, conjure.

Hear scrubbings, spud flesh, learning to steer the wheel to park parallel, tunes he sung for us alone in foreign tongues.

Croon your own maybelaters. Your sons will tell you that you say it each&every time they ask you. The worry of the warm lights on in the house of a cold, kept-up parental.

You forget the thin and starving thing you were. You could turn dumb and fevered, hardened, boiled, flood yourself a bathtub of blubber. You never wore a cover up.

(What were the names we once gave each other?)

There were notes he passed us nailed and taped to the bunk (hanging takes forever). There were hours we spent in mirrors, covering up, busts stuck small, yanks and tough tugs and wiggle-ups into older sister's on-loan nylons. Practice pursing fish lips, wearing dresses: an oyster iridescence. As we were punch bowls, spilling over, the gowns shone like slushes, the ones we grew once out of.

Memorize a rumor, a mole, the burn you heard about when he jumped off those dunes, the hit-twisted foot that lands and cracks, the bows that sealed your hairdos. Fishtailed braids do not unravel, but follow the gangly leader's heel to toe, heel to toe. Beach is beneath you. Have you danced since the I dos? Have you had bouts?

We were sisters with each other, onion weepers once we saw him, braiding maidens on the bleachers, all compeers, wanting to own him.

Us he spun. With us, there were ribbons on the roadside, there were donuts in our hands. There were nails on the lamppost, there were papers for lost dogs. We drew cards and straws and saw them as a sign that he was gone.

Now say *Beau.*

Fiancé.

Sea voo play?

Twist your ring. Say then, *ménage*. Now, *hors d'oeuvres, au revoir.*

In our kitchens, we are lazy susans on the other line, sipping pop through straws. We are trying to come up with something more than what we say to them about what it was.

Those names got old. We forgot.

We have seen it in our girls.

I Go to the Trees

My skin has nicks. There are languages, pages and numbers, stars and charts, all forbidden by Gram so foreboding then—oh dominion, mystique! The books are bibles, thick and noxious, hearty and weighty. Jehovah is unhappy with me.

Gram blabs of dark magic, says I do not believe.

Snakes! She says. Dangerous.

I am too young to get it—the priestesses and the religious agree. I wish were psychic, but still am no mystic. All old ladies are witches.

They say bedeviled! Possessed!

I hide catalogues under serpentine springs, coiling jagged and snagging my scripture. The pages worn, torn out, charged. I am made by quincunxes, septiles and planets. My knowingness singes the edges of pages up skyward. They curl beneath the covers. The texts are quilted: hideous, beaten.

A good harvest.

That is darkness, worship.

Almanac, I say to Gram.

I skip back to bed and uncover my creed, mesmerized by recitation—rites. I take blades to my sides to draw arrows, twins—oh, the sting! Would that I could sustain.

Saturnine children dare not be adorned in dark hues lest the devil might pick them for plagues, say they. I am sick with the dictums that sing to me, the pages infectious.

I sit through what they call the meeting, hauled to the

Kingdom Hall fuzzy and sleepy and sore from my Saturday scarring. I have listened too long to their tellings.

What sustenance is heretics? Disfellowship for transfusions, for cheating, for gambling or drinking.

I cannot say birthday without hisses—the elders, the littles. I get asked what for and what is this?

My birthday I ask Gram again and again to tell palmists my sign and my rising.

Winter, she says.

I need the certificate.

Lost it, she lies.

I am tired of the shouting, the shunning.

We march down the lanes, knock on doors. We leave papers in hands of neighbors who hate us. Pamphlets.

I sit outside classrooms while kids give allegiance. Not one intuits my lesions. I roll down my socks to see Neptune—ruler of undoing, colored sea blue in crayon. Draw a man in wax with fins to hook on my headboard. I will call him a fish to my Gram. Should she find him, I will not be nice.

It is not nice, says Gram, to be starry.

Press. The heat of the glyph flushes red. When I wash, I lock and unlock the brass knob. I do not let Gram in to talk. She knocks. Water runs. I make a splash.

You will prune.

Soon, I will get out. Hear this: I witnessed nothing.

Read me now—soothsayers, prophets, tarotesses! Oh, clairvoyants, if you only could give me my fortune. I would puncture my numbers and adorn them.

Moons and mercuries staining up my side, poison midheavens for liveries. Insignia of luscious Venus and martian birthmarks could deliver me.

You have heard our knocks. Were I you, I would keep the door shut.

There is a box of spilt papers, yellowdogs and there papers sit—signed by my mother. Should I have the natal hours, I should know which sign, but should Gram find me finding—I will not be nice. Oh, Jehovah.

I am a witch in my wishes, I am saying. There have long been locks betwixt the mattress.

In the dark, she pulls out her partial plate and brushes it clean. Its clinking is in the bowl. I have seen her mole on her nipple, have seen how her nose points arrowed out. I have seen how she lies, how she dyes her hair yellow. She cuts it up and cuts it off. She dabs her mole.

There is a glass on the sink where she soaks her fiddled-out gabber. I have put my fingers in it. In her mouth, on her tongue, there are bumps that make maps. That tongue is a sesquisquare—a biquintile. It makes a locomotive. In her holes, there are some gums. Way behind, there is silver and it chimes and it clanks our forks banging around in the back. There are metals. She is loud. There are sharp smells.

I have teeth to lose. I have taken her teeth, worn them in. Have lost some, put them beneath, betwixt my mattress. I have waited and nothing comes.

No coins and no bills. No fairies.

Pagan, says Gram. No Santa—he is of Satan.

I did not get pillow presents. I hid what fell. On my skin, I nicked Wicca spells.

Gram puts her partial plate in in the morning. In night, she takes pisses. I hear her up reading, hiding. I am slicing a node on my torso. Beneath go my bibles, my ologies, myths. She sees my lights on.

I nick.

I have laundered our linens. There are odors in her unders.

A knock is on the door. I make it dark.

You get to bed, she says.

I lie, I am.

The moon's yellow blinds me through the blinds.

Gypsies, they do not go knocking on doors. They do not go knocking on wood. They do not go rapping on glass, or tut-tutting. Mystics, they have birthdays, they have big rings, their wrists bemetaled. Mystics wear tangled hair in braids.

Gram says, Rat nest locks.

With the kitchen scissors, she cuts my hair clean off.

Now I look crooked.

Gram, she cut her hair to her ears when she chose the Truth. I want long hair, braids that coil and spring, long pigtails hennaed, unbrushed. I dig my locks out of the garbage, saved for Sabbats.

I go to the woods sometimes. I go to the trees sometimes to lean. Liber Linteus tells me when trees sponged up my full mooniness and made me go deeply, wild and unwell, I read. I lean on the tree and touch my fingers together. I take my fingernails to my belly and open up a nick and push down harder on the parts that are hairier. I do as I should not. Sometimes I scare myself by those trees.

The doorbells are what I would rather ring. Do you like for no names to knock at your place? This is why we are ding-dongs. They hate us. This is why.

Cults, they say of the coven.

I do not, in school, like how I must sit out. I do not like pageants where they all sing songs. Oh, to be alone on cold linoleum! To peer down the lane through the gates and see cakes! Service disservices. The thrust of oak doors closing is always old, unwelcoming us.

The lion face knockers I would not knock. Nor do I wish to knuckle oak. I do not like to look in the eyes of what we call the goats in the congregation. Goats, they do not know Jehovah.

Could we not leave them alone?

Listen—I am no pioneer. I have scrolls that show hemimoons crescent, waning and waxen. I have charts of the stars, the lists of switches. I have not knocked since Sunday. I would not knock again. I will tell Gram I will not. I would not scale the sidewalk pleading. I would not call that pioneering.

I will sing still my un-ode.

Are you familiar? I ask the families, the unholies.

I will render for them Armageddon. Listen. My heaven is in bed with my sect.

I will say no to the waters, to the tests. I will stay unbathed, take no baths. The baptism will not happen. I would sink.

Did they float in Massachusetts? Did they die, then? Oh, I would stay dirty, oily to reek of a conjuror, and aura.

I will say no to the elders. I will lie in bed on Sundays. I will stay in bed on Sabbats, my bibles surrounding.

Oh, to sleep in!

I would hide away from the doors with their deadlocks, curse the New World Translation.

Oh, to knock nevermore!

I have Ouija and tarocs, the Crowley. I turn a Celtic cross.

Jehovah is unhappy, says Grammy.

I flip the Devil, the Sun, reversed swords, a reversed wand. Spread spreads on my bedspread, spells, rapture. The smell is burnt herbs. I chant verbatim verse.

Do you know what they did in Romania? Bohemia?

You have shut us out. You have told us no.

We go back to our vehicles. Saturdays full of no-one-theres and not-homes.

She boils the water, Gram does. I have seen her pluck. The potions she has in bottles, her powders, make her look less witchish. Concealer on her moles pat and click compacts blare silver mirror, and she can see where she should use some rouge where there is pallor. Her perfume blooms reeky. She is saggy. She is leaky, leaving stains at the crook of her and on the ottoman. I have done the dirty linens, laundered.

I have seen her bleed like me. I found it between and looked for a rag, a tourniquet, something. The water dilutes it, but it spreads and swirls. I did not go see a doctor.

No doctors, no blood.

The trees are what I went to. I scare myself there in those woods when I leave. With my picking and plucking, I am bleeding and blaming Piscean rising for beaming down and yellow and making me leak. Oh, Jehovah, my father, the doctor, Mother and dog.

The chore of the rapping, the rousing.

Oh, to be alone!

I say my ode, On the cold.

The raised rhymes lighten when I repeat them. My fingers touch plush hushes of past Marches.

The spring stings me dizzier, ill with the whiles, the charms, incantations, the bewitchment, the chants, the charts, the jinxing, the hexing, the vex conjuration, the go, the tour, enravishments rumble, the lure, the lore, the rapturous canon, sacrosanct ascendants, the aspects, the cardinal Ariens, Cancerians, the Librans. Listen. I am speaking of zodiacal conjunctions, the Vedic, the Venusian, the modes and the moons, numerologic, ephemeris, descendants, decans, orbs, horary, nakshatras, grand crosses, squares and M. coeli. I am moved by mutables, not without ruinous runes, fixeds, triplicities and trines, rods and wands, transits and querents, discs and pips. I would not stop at progressions, part of fortunes, divinations, cartomancy and diviners, retrogrades, the page, the signifiers.

What is the wish but to have?

I know names for the ways to do cards. I know stars.

We are knuckleheads knocking.

I have my pack, my *calendario*. There are my sages.

What of my nascence? I cannot say. There is pain. There is only carving a day out, one after the other and dissimilar.

There is only digging where there is what I have. What can be done is nothing but flushing. Now, there are smelling salts and salves for the made. My birthmarks. There are starfuls of sky, of my etchings. There is Gram in her maybes and she is sleeping. She has bleached it, the peach fuzz.

Was it a dealing Diablo? What was it—the canon tornado that did it? Who would give this to a girl as I am? I have numbers, coordinates and horoscopes. I have archers skidded on my hip—nicks.

What it was not is how now I am made. What girl could go on? From mat to mat. Up one step, down one step, the way how dogs go. The doors of the dogs go clacking and waving unweighty. Their tails wave us away. Not one has licked my hand.

These ankles at my age! Old soul who swole—I am this and my nicks. The resting bangles, hoops and these hollers. I have stars and charts and marks and nicks and Gram did warn me. She told me not to husk about the day, the date, the age, the minutes, positions, did tell me do not! Do not! Did tell me pagan and Satan and Satan. She did say to me praying her interpretation. She took out her teeth that did rot away woodish. She bled and I cleaned. I did all her linens. My linens filled with feral illness.

I scare other kids. I scared off Ma, deadened and blooden, and I did slurred lunar dances tuneless, endless until the sun resurrected.

The lapis of crayons themselves drew themselves out. I danced with the crayon a bad dance, a Neptunian. Gram prays to Jehovah God toothless.

The branches get snippy. I am the twig from her limb. The wind wound the kaftans around and I fit her rigid, red set to my tongue. I tasted her sayings. I fit her teeth, put them in my mouth.

I just did it again.

Cursed myself.

Damned.

Beige

The taste of an ear is some guess I arrive at. Think, though, of wan carnivals, blah stalls. White out your look.

Look inside your hardware.

Memorize woolen hats.

Drive hourish earlier to park nearer, settle, wander, go for a mug, mirror brown eyes with the rear. Used to be no car, so rode a bus to cemented interiors. Employed in the duff of a dungeon, every beige paned the wall.

See flesh stale, dishwater color, my closet expectant with dresses, dresser drawers hold nudes, muted panties, tan hose. That was October. I wore beige, glared notice.

Scabrous cubicles were carpeted where fester rendered. I was braying my legs, grasping. I wait my turn, bear as I can.

Gyre forward.

Hands crimp rodent devices, undo, undo, draping the pause in a render to show you motion. Picture proposal under arm, the stubble incidental.

Used to be no car, so staid. Awaited a bus. Late for meetings, staying across from myself. Faked a yawn, scanned the schedule against a crude poll. Tried hard to leak you, handing loaves up as thank-yous in the break room.

Kept yeast occasionally. But, know what? Loafing foiled, so we might misstep throated scowls.

In pink, it said, Name. One piece baked with my beige. Before breath starved. Trim gristle, said you of revisions.

(Cutting celluloid tinges displeases what makes spots good.)

Pack a lunch.

So, we will stay then?

Missed the mark, Ms.

When you piecemeal, marinade on this, linger. Weep over sizes and squeal over borders and reset to 1080i. Moonlight stages accidents. All night in the tank, splice and listen for dialogue.

Start hearing, Come near me.

My tights squeezed too tight. Too shovy to peel thigh-highs. Went home solo. I cannot suck an itch.

When we flickered together in beige, and the slight of your brining me misconstrued space, disabled with predictions of bed aged the tumbler all night, neighed tongue-tied lulls, dreamt us wide, waked under comforters and sewn up dull. This makes for all the right music.

What want!

Yes.

Where your mind went then.

I pin these to pizzicato stucco. Diagrams of how to shoot with a Hague, who to speed dial for surround sound. Go home and plank your hands sticky. Steam up third floor door, wash my beige.

Lapses happen often. Missing rings.

Broiled conglomerate must be addressed. I view ways how to frame shots, of how it looks when you take off your hat. Memorize woolen caps looking into my shoes. You shook snow.

I wish a blizzard for machines, the cameras, make us sleep beige on beige.

Indent. Your skull must taste woolen. One night a bus will not come.

You stutter, a fly in tongues. I seep what I seek.

Wisconsin, the Man

The Grout

Looking at myself in her mirror, my mother's, I note our shading is hollowing— the extremities, our proximity.

I remain uncertain you could call what she has given me life.

Had I been known to be disloyal to her?

Imagine the lobby of a gilded motel. She sat beside a man who was very much not my father. His insistence on my cuteness grew suspect. He set faint minuets of tiny martinis before me. The flavor was deficit of any integrity.

We began with faux pas. I noted he shared a birthday with the Führer. The man laughed far but hardly.

Then, the telephone, the ringing flits had me holding the thing arms' lengths away, shades from my ear. Her phrases glimmered. They were dabbed at to excuse her due to turbulence.

Paths in the sky had errored. I was not to undermine.

I took issue with fuselage that summer where the flowers overlooked living, earthworms swole excessive with weather. Later, they lay curdled solo in dim, concrete cracks. The first flight I took seated me beside a guy who was half in my lap playing like a former pro, a captain passing me cards with shadowed lettering.

The woman is itinerate. Her cells were cement. I was to forge her name near the *x* to save room for two.

She showed through when she tumbled into window menus of eloquent restaurants. She had come on her tongue.

Her habitual rambles I could incant were inexact: she over-said shit like, Life's good.

Could you see the diffidence, the slow reveal of the angle, how I sat, slang on the leather, how it stuck against my razor burn, the redness, my haunches?

The Lobby

Mother brings a man along. Along comes the man. She—polka dotted, frilly, underdressed.

He is a man she hears nothing about.

The voice of her mother on the telephone hummed higher. Her attired mother, a briefcase lady sings the sound of the tumbler cut with bracelets. She drank a drink just.

The man asked how was it.

When you were born?

Why do you ask?

Oh, stars.

I ask you give me the month.

A man who was turning darker colors at the head as if he were a man from only his button-up. The tumbler spun stomached, and she felt like her mother looking at herself, making a grown-up sweat.

All around is gold, papers stuck up to the wall with the finest solvents. There is talk of competition regarding relishing. Celery slurs in their cups, swirls dumb and crunching.

All around is a black and white tune shooting up pianos. This is a place where they pay the player. The bill is not Dutched. The man is unkempt, says he will shave for his soirée while we go bumming. The man has not so much as stubble.

She nicked her leg in the tub that day. She rubs the dry bud. She turns her wrists wide, circles middle to thumb.

Unbecoming.

(The unwashed plates, pans, each arachnid still, the doorbell that did not ding, they would call the dinger the ding-dong, the knocker the knocker, the lock, the lip with the hair, the rips of the wax that removed it, the sting of the bleach that blondes it, the now bitter milk hid away in doses, the ribbons she slid from fine hair, receipts in the lining, a pocket Caesarean, pins slipping into the undone hem, dull nickels, yellow discipline slips.)

Suddenly I am the Pancho Villa Of

I am spotted with a haircut growing out disillusioned by its pontification and rebellious corks. I have earned a spotted bladder from indignity to hold my piss as I begin to give her the business.

Was it pertinent we meet?

The Girl Shakes Herself

The drinks are on him, were for them—the mother and girl. The mother has the money, but he says it's on me.

Sit still.

The girl shakes her leg, does not sit still.

How'd she take it?

Blonde, says the mother.

He was, the mother says, the man from Wisconsin, and the nodding daughter knows who she means, bows her head, takes his hand between hers, and he gives a dead fish. Her hands handle him with business.

What's wrong with her? asks this man.

Our habit, Mother says.

The girl tangles her knees and the mother says, Stop. Set.

Tangos unhinge, dangle through the door slits of those who resorted. She turns white at what she sees between.

An old soul, said the mother to the man. Laughs unalike.

The run stays in the girl's legs and taps at Wisconsin, the man. She pulls at the man's hand, lines sidewind. She has seen ugly.

The Man From Wisconsin

Same as she wound my headache with a comb, she held me by the hair.

She came to see me to say she would, in her way, be leaving, tergiversated the table even as I said, Wait.

I was buttered up. Some big shot chef's *hors d'oeuvre* place. Over a meal that was over a zillion yen. Oh, over oak-aged goblets of Sauvignon Blanc, she told me she had had it, rebooked her return.

Once, she was a person who was nervous, who drank to fly on planes. I ate what she ordered. I sampled the gravest mistake.

Are they known to go bad?

Just taste them, just try them.

They were shimmering, poisonous things.

I do not crave sea fare upon the cement, their iridescence. I watched her tell me this time she means it, no funning.

Who is he?

Oh, you know.

This is something she openends.

A man —

Names were named.

She paid the bartender, the landlord. She paid the driver. She tipped the bellhop.

She tipped the man in the elevator, paid off, at home, the babysitter. She bought the tickets, the dresses, insurance, the passes, the hairdos, tuition, the luggage, my aprons and cups, my bowls and my spoons.

I had had an allowance.

She paid James. It was too hot to speak of: the scald, the concrete. It was some tundra to which we belonged before we left. We lived in this pale house with a wood floor, and she gave her all to her tests, her fasting, her figure.

She was my mother, thin hair, middle-thick.

Corporate Financial Officer. Be consistent.

It was thwapping rulers. It was ledgers that howled back, upset stomach midnights. It was one-room palaces, maple syrup, learning about spiders — the eight eyed.

She paid to brace me. I have the teeth of a crook. Can't think too hard about it, the way that that metal bussed, the way babies teethe.

So I was told. About the plains. How he would like to patronize a museum. How he could do it for himself.

It was the talking, I assure you.

A stamped card said when I went home there would be no house, the bon fires would be scoffed. There would be soot. There would be no kids. I would not have the gravel.

I came out a debutante.

It was the horror of summer, its cursive hours.

Autobiography of the Mere

I live with a girl named Elizabeth who is about to build the same year for herself as I did.

I am subletting from a go-getter. I host the scenario. I say copious I-don't-knows to a faux homeroom. We apply abroad to teach the English language. Our accents compete.

She proposes herself to the state. She stares deep into herself in the microwave while the soup spins around. Our chore is being good and bringing keys along. That's adding up the home we can't get back.

What heeds a thousand walks? Go bother everyone with updates. Make your someone sorry. A long-form sorry.

I hum myself blank.

This is the year we trash our blankies. Now, we are cast to be wearing jewelry, to improve the mood quietly.

The accomplished are among us. Who, smiling at screens, are genius hyperboles. We live amongst a number of congratulated blonde temples. Whoops: I socialize. Sorry about that verb. I always sink appropriately or hop in your lair groggy.

Walk until you sleep. Vex us less serious.

I take a loss since I can't believe.

People fuck up when they try. Will my bed bugs remember me? We have broken furniture by accident. Not to cross any martyrs!

What if my cause was to stop every drinker from making powdered lemonade? I just want us rolling lemons on the floor with dirty feet. Stay a softie. I can't succeed based on cleverness. I have fallen out of love with my cell phone.

Silence your bowel movement or else face the judge. We are such forts for our shit. What a world!

I would love to be taken captive. Force the thought. I wasn't captivated. I had captivated someone and so you know, they physically took me captive.

Now, I'm in the witness protection program. What that is, is I live at this house.

Activate, Elizabeth, breathily. I like her goodbyes, that she has on an outfit.

I like laughing at lightning in bed.

I'm trying to stay with this notion of afloat. I don't mean to sound better by putting an "a" there. I do mean, though, to convey the wonderful feeling of light that comes with underwater somersaults, something conveyed to my assailant when he began hand-feeding me thickish turkey reubens as he starved, watching—swished colas over his teeth. Waiters couldn't fill the glass fast enough, his excuse to tip low.

Our other roommate I've met is a real prick. She saw those fat pics from high school of my twin brothers and I over the desk and bets were off in getting her to stammer out more than a, You left your keys in the door again. I also do that. She was chasing me down avalanachishly. I was hungry for us both.

I take a lot of supplements as of late. Elizabeth, I make myself drink salad instead of looking for a new boyfriend. I sleep with my things against the door, then pack back up. I pack and repack the van. Words get lost in the letters of the move. The stiller people sour—it's not something I want. I honestly feel longer than the fourth meal. The motion also worries me. I'm afraid I'll be tired and won't have a place to sleep. I've been afraid of that since remembering I was awake. My mother was waking me up in the core of night to assemble egg rolls.

I'm afraid of the pink juices you mix up for yourself for health use because I relate very much. You're reusing your bottle, I see. You're the most protected in the photograph of the never-fraught four of you—you each look vibrant against the radiator, as should be, and like absolute achievements. That's one thing, Elizabeth. I don't photograph well. Other girls do great tricks with their feet in a *releve* position, but I generally go to the bathroom, well, because I pee quite a lot and also because the composition of a friendship photographed has also always made me feel captured as opposed to captivating.

I talk to myself in the bath to try to make reason before meet ups. I don't like seeming demure, so I say this to the mirror. Ever wonder with the radio button bellowed to one side so you can't get out, which sometimes means pressing a pedal down to the floor in park to practice for the real thing I threaten?

Dumb Math

Used to be you could tell which one you were looking at—the riddle didn't leave me with any feeling toward which wrist. I meant to match this swatch: what crawled the beach to wreck its signs. If no one came home after Ma, we would know to hold our hands in our laps.

Why would you wear hose to drive in all day? Ma asked me this before she went. I said I like how they keep holding me in.

I sense the couch staring blank ahead like it's super sorry. Our meals scoop out tasteless, lukewarm at best. I remember our sweet roll allowances, leave out the whole trashed oven. The frosting spilt, smelling black, tastes of char and sugar.

I had itchy metal braces. For fun, I was drowsy with allergies. The waves came in to nuke PBJ ooze. I took fingers to scoop it beside the computer. The wind blew in around midnight. I would be showing old men parts of my body.

One told me he would take me from my family. He was living with his loving father. He dialed me up when I faked sick to touch it awhile. He made honest noises. I got nothing from it, just knowing. I thought I could live a life of hostels.

When the men saw what I sent, it was better than being taught. I failed Algebra a lot. I was passing as a forty-five year old who wrote a screenplay called *Thirty Six Hours of Sunshine.* His hair hung to his privates. I was doing great talking with two Kentucky bis. The lazy eye one was saving his money to get fixed up. The other was allergic to the sun.

Ma made me change hot diapers for my mouth running.

I knew all about how a mouth could hurt. I learned my psychosis from a library book, could feel what was next in my wrists.

On field days, they gave ribbons even for sitting out. Shit at being wheelbarrow? They passed you for coming.

Here came the casseroles. At first, I did not know why I was allowed to eat. I ate my whole life up until then. Here I held on to Formica, flushed my meals.

This is strange, but in that age I bled every day of the lunar month. My teeth hurt and bleeding hurt. I had nothing to say, no room to remark. Even songs tiptoed out of my mouth. I liked the impact. I was afraid someone would run me over. I could just see headlights. Sometimes the moon came out so early. I was blue-green with nausea from all I was losing. Swallowed snot. I liked to listen for my steps through the woods. I liked the sound winding backwards. I liked to think about bouncing off trees. No one was awake when I stamped in sludge, performed algorithms.

I got put in dumb math. When people asked, I wanted to fib.

Why is this happening? I would ask Ma, and she would not have much of an answer. I cried above my dinner when I passed the salt and pepper. She would tell me I was scaring the babies. If I ran away, my braces would be stuck there with my gums growing over the top. I did not believe straight teeth made somebody good looking.

I did not believe the answer keys.

Those Who Have Dwelt in My Lilt

So few have dwelt in my lilt that I reign in the remainder. This tale will irrepressibly smell of holes. At lights out, our lives—yours and mine—echoes guesstimates. Others' seats are my fave I feel for, for piddles cool slow, alone.

Interstitially, I floor. I aim for inducing sneezing to stick a digit in twinky sphincters.

Ah! Dwell, dwelled, dwelt.

I meant to enbalm ya'll in swoop-ins. These odes I ooze!

Today, I introduce myself most lucidly to you via whoopses.

Many asked before they had felled, Are you from somewhere elsewhere?

Some infer my skin is prepared at the specialty grocer a town over with the copious consonants, for the very middle of me revealed isn't certain, is powerfully splotched.

Serious businesses, their stylized front windows—each have eeked this forayed display you conceive. All mirrors, integers and signatures go slant by I.

Amidst equinoxes, I pace, wrack up telephone minutes, fool around with rooms. Ever I have slummed indoors. When I unroll hosiery, a grokky mayo peeps from having failed at a forage. The animal kingdom potlucks towards the lawn ornaments. They hoard my sighs in delight as I spread picnics in my living room.

Whom of us' doom isn't made of such charcuterie?

Harshities

Bucolics

Brother

He woke searching in his ears. Too many reptilian servings, spouse toes, techno strangers under rented rooms made him croak. He will if the scratch off snuffs, no one to say it to. He likes to see women tortured by pleasure in porn.

He is mad about the room, the ring, his virginity. He was entitled to something since he had not much beyond what he overate, never having gone off to college. Metallic wrists promise boyhood from blood. He blames failure on the garaged pleasure he shared with boy neighbors.

He did it to a girl and he was sorry. She had kidney stones to pass. They parted on a hill and in her dreams fell down them. He offered tokens, had once taken her places bucolic, what sprung out the locus of her.

They share a home as financiers. There are bitsy rats the feline drained. Their ancient rug comes from a highway store in Sault Sainte Marie, where they wet their beds. Women with permanents sold it with its fur and amniotic splash.

She puked in the bath with him. He was too big to fit. In photographs, they were head near head, quesadilla eaters. His penis was indifferent to adults—he appreciated toenails painted faint colors, the sandaled young.

Dad told her it's time to start shaving down there. Legs too, Sweetie. Mom was asleep early. He took his hand to the soft of her under-knee.

The ritual brought her her maker. He shaved his beard how she saw Aunt Cecilia do. She walked with no cure. A certain type of bug started living in her house and waiting with her while she clinked the little mixture.

Do they make the dosage cups plain so you don't stray dark and large? The burning of some cigar against sweet faces. She rarely kept the cap on. Dead woman yogurt on the cover.

The eggs boil, keep company. She put them to time the twitches of the coming along and the lotion for that. People in commercials have procedures on the beach. They cum.

Electrocuted, the hairs on her belly growing in, Chablis got the gall. Small trimmings skuzz her razors. No one saw she washed. Short shorts made an abrasion between, so she felt second best, ate less and tumbled around holding onto her stomach.

Her brother too troubled his follicles. He took all off before finding a fuck. Let other boys know he thought that gross. The drain was plugged by him.

On the train, he fucked me with a spatula. He didn't feel much from cunt. We moved around loud on either side to replace gun sounds. I used his butter up.

We picnicked atop a two by four; he squeaked at the woods. The ants inside my mouth stepped around his cock. I told him things said in movies by sociopaths. He smiled, irrelevant and satisfied.

The Ruler

The landwoman hated the Bangledeshi next door. Downstairs, the New Yorker jammed her house. The daughter shouted at her on the sidewalk. They are always ringing my doorbell, and I am in the middle of saying fuck.

He had others over to drink drinks and pretend they could smoke a cigarette. They say you could see her shape through a towel. The apron I wear protects me from psychics. I do cooking only after noon when I've had my coffee and killed a few bugs.

They stay still and wait with me for the next right amount of pause. There are bed bugs all about where a moustache would be. Don't you want to be golden and safe? I think, Can't I?

Hors de Combat

My bedroom is hotter than his. I go to his floor like a sidekick. He doesn't know the difference between a molding sponge and over-inflating young ladies. The sensation is sweaty, disposed.

He lies in bed until supper, pounding expensive smoothies. We worship insanely and not each other. Collective hummings cosign our brood. We risk kindness.

He sleeps toes up. His pipes digest. The water stays trapped, mixed with the false chemical smell of men sloshing. At my bath, my feet scummy, peeling, we worship indifferent frequencies.

His sister hurts herself in ways most legitimate. Over-exercising gifts her with limp health, tawny advantages. Still, she wants to work in a mall, selling to people who slight, seeming lithe, like they're having an elusive, controlled time. I watch these two, and the bitter stuff that brews in the kitchen flows through me straight to dung.

You learn to know the difference between what you fuck. In the summer, jobless, waterlogged, you search your timid keratin. Itch your sun insults. Total avoidance from the high school foes you leaned on and fell over.

I never told ole brother where I'd go. He took dumps on the Lord. He tinkled his clandestine inclusions. I hated his gestalt.

I never said that I went to get shot nude. The guy was lisping away, insisting on his girlfriend's total participation and advisement in his taking photos of people cutting onions, sprinting, crying mid-jism. She was inside the frigidity of the bathroom, punching at her arms naked. I interrogated the whole bitch.

I couldn't find love for her or puppies after. I'd go to galleries and to the store. I'd make myself a miniature dog. I watched them roll and pant into the Plexiglas.

Off to a mermaid parade, tar tore my sandals. My hobbles burped about. Re: hospitals—I budgeted none. I used my tank top for a shoe.

Runt Suction

I taught myself to suck off my tits. I was getting thinner, so it got harder to yank my nipples up toward my teeth. Anything is discounted if you wait. The ingredient was whatever I could afford.

The day hiccupped. I ate prepacked two-buck sausage. Missed the musical to fall ill in a park and listen to a blogger go on. He was a chore.

You see the shit you say? You met a celeb. That's you? Nope.

I'm past upset. You think I'm interesting? I bought your shitty chips. That money's due.

I want to nap in your debt. Stop your jaw until the money from that sangria drink is pouched. Stop talking vegetarianism. Listen, Carrot Suck, discuss celebrities when we settle.

That night was loud and insensate: self-intercourse and thunderstorms. I got home, cut my callouses, avoided my roommate and plotted my irrelevant death. I tried eighty types of rice pudding to cope. I finally made the pet infestation call.

Rats here and now larvae, fleas, maggots and fat friends at home who refused to do a dish. The moment I arrived, I would smash up the kitchen. I would take the pests, crush them into something I'd call a black bean burger. I'd feed these fucks.

Proposition: I'll play beer pong when you de-clit your babygirls. This is how I feel about culture—this. The only answer for me is to rage with millionaires training for marathons in perfect shape. It was I who did it.

It has been trying for him to meet girls online. When I got home to see my future husband, the documentarian, he took me out for runny steaks and told me he slept with "mulatto prostitutes." I lost an organ.

If everything is charred you surround people, asking. If, watch a DVD, the spoiled yellow that pops out in the dark behaves for you as mild, thin upstate girls. You are worth so much to yourself you never realize when you lose. Nothing aids digestion.

Toomsuba

I am fond of onyx so much I would work to have things.

In the duration of this state, I was born on a Sunday. Everyone recites my birth certificate gorged on sty, ridiculed while donning raincoats. I drove them bats, emptied buckets of myself out smallish windows, bordered versions of live-in friends. Here I fell out of a schizoid self-rated first favorite self. When it got bad, it helped me cross the road. I took to pants. I ate ala mode. I started to get into it with a girlfriend. Then, her cunt said, Nope.

On any of these nights, I could have stayed home. Instead, I spread butter on the breads and smacked each end as if the two of them quarreled, then belonged. I belabored my pots and pans to feel whole, and they burned warped for me to parent, sink-wash, scrub. I seek myself out to masturbate. They say you gotta ask.

I loot the pantries of parties I feel uninvited to. I got to be a person who never winced goodbye. My room's my brain. I stay dim. I call people over so I go clean.

An Ode to the Well-Traveled

I chose a pretty little ring covered in sparkles to remember my travels. The next train to the next destination, the metal tumbled to the tiles and echoed under the sands beneath people's feet. The thing became noise.

I bought a replacer in a shop close to the station. Its blues and chartreuses tinkled speckles. A sound rang out of a late anorexic, the shrill again. I thought those bitches whispered. I tossed my hand in the air to catch myself. The trinket split into twiddled minutes.

The final momento I took out of my ears and left on the nightstand. They were poking me while I sought a fuck.

I commissioned a tattoo of the perdurable look on my face, a portraiture line for line, which most tsked. This lasted until my third sojourn. I wore a bandage to cover the hole where my ink used to lie. It grew into my skin. I itched out the dressing and a cream came forward. Now I drink punch.

Snippets

I got robbed. Now I am out for a dainty lunch. My roommate is blaming me that we were broken into: the bare ass window. She leaves her underwear all over the living room, sets intuitive traps. Don't mention this because she might stop. I don't think thieves quit thieving. They just want to be around her.

Then, I erased all of the confirmation I was given that you were on my side. I climbed and thought of the word ascendant and how you appear to others. If I gave birth to you that would make me trust you. Prick—IVs up my arm, where the prison of the head skips to the aviation inclined.

I harp to my bedside knives we should not take stock.

We chug until the click gets our eardrums. We require malleable skies, mind plastic gorges.

Another Section

You are no star. This is the city; knight it and call bullshit. The silver can bear, can follow you vomiting of autumn, buffoon to the thumb. You are no barrel glean on me.

You have to see it like: here it is, I get purpose from it. I'm stolen from home, and they can't wait until I get going. I'm there just to get them from place to place, a freighter at the border.

Toomsuba

Daddy was watching his sports. I loved staying in the green room with the carpet, ruining my hands over the rough. I only do a couple of things okay, but I think I'm a good listener. Call you quiet. Call you house mouse or damsel—yank you anywhere, to a store where they need wipes. You start to get packed in. This isn't a corral. I'm done with this cart pushing business. It started out I was stuck in there with my legs lifting. Now I got the missus' list.

I'm not to be told. You talk too much. You shower too much. You think aloud, and it pierces my ears. There isn't a way for me to respire. There aren't, through fields or farce, flowers to sniff at, sneeze, not any water for me without bodies encased into beiges like chicken and pork. Worse yet, the color when oil gets against the ground and still rises.

You're Breaking Up

The continental and obligatory morning meal pecked at for reasons of inclusion. Various back and hither about potentiality with concern to apparent dong swingers, distracters. He hangs from her rearview, pollutes conversations, if this is what they could be called, to concern in chief, their quote telepathy unquote or the mega meaning of the two of them fighting and fucking like the rest of us sore of gum occasional smokers. Dogs snap when I try to clip their nails. I guess I wouldn't oblige getting my ass wiped for me either.

Now, I'll describe setting: the rats run across power lines. Daddy's piano rotting in the backyard.

You want a story, sleep in. Draw from your dreams.

My Given Name

I went looking through a herd to find my husband. He got stationed away, and I came looking after his body, didn't know where to ride the trains to find his tags, his head separate.

Sand is something I put inside myself never knowing—incubation of a sororal and sub-similar earth. I went to a doctor off base when I skipped so many months. He hit a bat so it broke to smithereens. I woke. He wheeled out toast. I couldn't get off the sofa.

I hate myself for telling him no when he'd take to below my belly. I told him it tickled, but I stayed numb, I suppose, and wanted not to be a lover for a while, just a wife. Our flowers froze. Our ghosts came in drafts. They drew us from bed. I stood on our steps and pissed against the cold.

Do I keep his name?

I'd go on writing checks to the lessor. I'd have to take a job and stay called Mrs. Him.

Never did smoke, but I got into the ritual of the match and asking for lights to lock eyes with, flickers of grins.

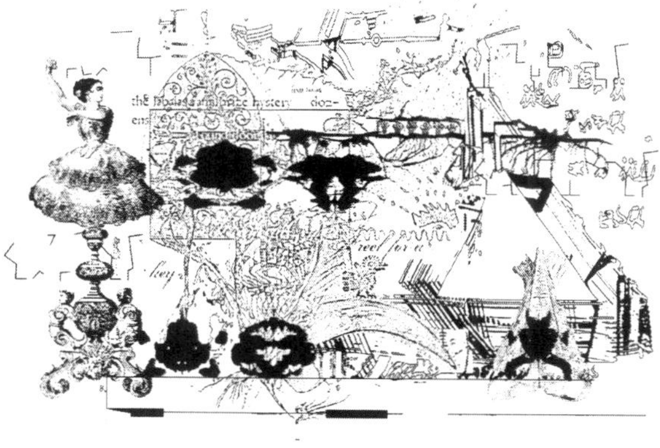

The Slumber Partier

I let bathroom doors stay open to feign affection, hoping the host might listen, but I'm afraid to seem like this crazy Lisbon acquaintance. Touring others' parlors, I try any noise my body won't choke or pass judgment. I sit in the dark where he stays. Meaning I'm made to shunt my spine. His pillows are the ones tossed off. I've been set out the flat shit.

I tuck to the corner of the pouted pullout on my way hurricaned through someone else. What I do appoints a flop. And worse, parties keep you abreast of misgivings. Most of my hosts have their say. I heard the salacity of the wink, slept perhaps a word. Some soak their feet in salt to suck out stress while I sit outside, but I think of this little liar who told me she was allergic to salt when I tried to feed her a piece of homemade pizza. I can't manage the hypochondria of my hosts squirting cummish purifications across their palms, making the same strained faces as I hand them obligations, gifts incessant, insistent. They fear matter may pollute their systems. They don't delight in remnants. For instance, said parties have tip calculators. I have marveled, swatted their devices, doubled the ten percent math, trashed their keeping-track trapper keepers, the crackers.

I can't stand for the way the public decides to sanitize. Those who gorge on corn syrup. Why am I always high-fived goodbye?

I habitually spilled honey on the stovetop of my then inamorato. He shouted and punished up a rag. He would excuse himself, huffy, shave his dome, scrape the razor scum, door secured. If you are still awake, I should confess to being grounded because the potty got stopped up with me. I never plunged. From the pile grew sleek tomatoes.

I did once per month mention the boxes: geography, hill countries, biomes of needless cords and deciduous forests from once-constructed papers for purposes he lost. No room to rest sans a chair. The conversation went as such: a collage of overlarge hypotheses of why mauve. There was little space for me to meddle, spread my usual façade. That is, play house. We were lessees. He finagled the paints. I mean we were typed as those who think splishy-splash matters, hueing as fuel for the opposite of intercourse. His floor stayed hard.

My on-deck lover's powder room pounds my pounds equated about worth and idioms far worse. We indulged in cinematic banal anal, French girlfriends. He owns but one lamp, a sea fish attachment allowing phrases to be made in the pitch. He longs to make circles inside me so I snooze. This goo-goo eyed goon dry humps under the chemiluminescence. Never an aspiration among the upright. I trip over his barbells, piss the water he pours me, knees allowing his penlight. A terrible babysitter.

The evening makes everything its richer sophisticate. Please excuse me and I had hoped you would not have minded that I was feeling like I was having to get on going, I say. Blame dawning on for why. Better trek happier trails that would seem I was myself as I am wont to hide. Where I'd end up another stop.

Never The Boys

He says I want to hear a foomp when those panties drop. Jesus *Christ*.

I warn you, it gets ugly when I let it. My hips will cuss you out.

Like a jungle gal. Yay/Nay?

His magazines he mistakes as ladders are his dad's. They estranged in tiers. I wasn't with him when he dug for them, but I heard the story. Before, he would head to estate sales looking for photos of the now-deceased queens physically wide. The tawn of each page, the stiff, sticky paper used to be a gloss you could get to know. When he was on retreat, I tilted from the thick of his carpet and stirred these strumpets.

The first time he saw me bare, we were mid-calf in stacks middling the kitchen. My yellow boots dawned on his lawn that Spring.

He didn't bring up other hair. He balded young, in the era where I mastered grammar, but I never said bald to him. I maneuvered through the boudoir practicing superstitions. I rang angry that he forgot an aforementioned outing. I say it from my grit like a deer in the room.

Why in the hell wouldn't you save it?

Well, have you *seen* the crotches of late?

Since when?

The hair amounts. Hair is stubborn. I wish the shadow would bleach. I need to bleach my arms, my lip. I have to bleach the divot between my bra.

My mother stressed the ritual.

You must pluck what is under.

She hitched my chin in her pinch. Hands so small she can barely carry a bottle. She contended my head toward the mirror and shone a light on hairs. I got her worst parts. Out came tweezers I hissed at.

You might sneeze.

I did not dare for her to be right. In my nose, I held the sneeze. She's got claws: long and perfect and curved. I snotted about, a spray with leagues. Got her in the mouth, didn't regard her sorry.

You have to shave it all, her moustache crowning closer.

There's waxes with the home kits. Start saving for electrolysis.

I always shower, door locked, alone. She hid in the linens and wrestled me buck.

You did a sloppy job!

And she's looked into my vagina.

She nipped my hairs between her teeth.

Honey, check so your period won't wad.

There sat some chunks in said fauna.

Snackage, said he.

Now, be shooshed before you dismiss this as another dame excusing why I take so long in the john.

A woman never shits alone. This gentleman routinely wagged his no-no in my face unwelcomed as I shook loose a number two, composing this piece.

Mucker

Because Mik was a son, Mik wanted a son.

Because Mik wanted a son, he shot.

Because Mik wanted a son to skate, Mik chose what Mik wanted to choose—chose shoot, chose stick, chose puck.

•

Because Mik grew up in a town.

•

Because Mik went to States and won, but it's not on goal, nice shot, no snot on glove, no dose, doze, those skates, remember rinks with ice nosed blades.

•

Oh, sore, am I ever?

Because Mik cant zamboni away marriage marks.

Because Mik cant take off his skates.

•

Because when Mik walks, he walks laced up in old Bauers, does this even in off-season.

Because Mik ate a shitton on Sunday. Because he ate less all other days. Because he fine-dined at Ginos on salad bars, meatballs, white rolls, spaghetti, baked, marinaraed. Because he fine-dined on sticks, on pucks on punched-in fuckers, teeth skating out of their mouth. Because he hung around.

•

Because the brothers serve beers there.

Refrain.

Because Mik means hockey, somewhere hockey means Mik, and Mik means business.

•

Because he meant in grade one what he said when he said in grade one to a teacher who asked Mik,

Favorite color?

Black.

Why?

Puck.

•

Because Mik chose puck.

Because he shoots, he scores.

Because Mik says equipment and he means it.

Because Mik says blade and means it.

•

Because Mik says coach, means father.

Because Mik says meat and means it, too, he means meat when he says Sunday and win when he says play.

•

Because you gotta be hungry for it, says Mik.

Because Mik means what Mik says.

•

Refrain.

•

Because Mik was raised by the bay.

Because Mik was raised by the rink.

Because Mik grew up in his town.

Because Mik knew what he knew what he know of was this—puck, stick, ice skate, rinks.

Because he knew what he, Mik, was made of.

Because Mik knew the taste of rubber. Because Mik was missing teeth.

Because Mik was hungry morning noon and night for it, had teethed on this biscuit and it tasted like rubber and it tasted like metal and blood, puck and black, his favorite color.

Because Mik knew late locker room beers, borrowed chew and knew numbers, knew Bulldogs, knew drills and recruits. Because he knew brothers of brothers positions and knew looky look drills that buses full knew.

Because Mik had trophies, spoils and tokens and Mik had had wives but still had his spoils and medals and tokens and Mik still has skates that he's wearing right now.

●

Because Mik was both captain and coach. Because when Mik says captain, he means brother, says coach and means father.

●

Because he, himself, looked in the mirror. Because Mik met the blonde and decided he would have her.

●

Because Mik wanted the blonde.

Because Mik wanted the puck, chose the puck.

Because Mik chose pucks and sore am I ever?

Refrain.

Because Mik can't zamboni away those marriage marks, cannot sleep since, cannot stay, still, bad luck, back, bad fall, bad injury from the sticks or from the smash into boards cannot sleep, cannot sleep from sports channel TV blare, den dimmed, dark cans of pop spit chew, in after scrimmage, take off helmet says Mik.

Because, because.

Refrain.

●

Because his mother had four sons and one daughter, daughter wed a player as soon as she could and as soon as she could left the bay for a town over, much older, married a right wing.

Because Mik's mother had six brothers, mother of Mik, wife of Mister Mik had four sons and one daughter (Mister Mik called Boomer had one brother, Mik, and Mik had two Mik sons and Boomer, Mik, had four Miks, four sons and one daughter and the town started to call him Mister Bob or Robert and they called Mik Mik and they called the other sons, of Boomer, of Mik's mother, Mik and Mik and Mik and these Miks were Mik's brothers, locals said oneada, meant one of the Miks), they did not call the one daughter Mik. Because Mister Mik, dad of her, called her Poppy and Mik and Mik and Mik and Mik called her Sister.

●

Because Mik was a son, he was a Mik. Because he was, Mik would look at the sons on the ice and think brother or later thought son, would go home to the den and think dinner.

●

Because when Mik thought about dinner, he meant he was hungry for it, made dinner happen to him by dialing a number that began with four eight two or eight seven depending on what side of the bridge, could sing off key this son of subs he would press the code Sundays for his big dinner. Because Sunday is the big day Mik eats.

Because before skating, Mik wanted dinner.

Because dinner was what kept Mik going.

Because you gotta be hungry for it.

Because Sunday is the day of Mik.

Because Sunday is Mik's day of r & r.

Because Sunday sometimes means a game is on the sports channel, the den dimmed dark. After skating a game is on after the game.

Because (sore) he won't answer the phone if it rings but the phone is beside him—in case.

Because Mik does not want to miss a call or have to get up form the recliner unless to piss or shit, will spray canned spray smell over the stink, drops what he does not want to look at, will flush two three times if need be and if need be will shower with mug butt coiled, dons skates still, on blades, greening copper rust, they stay on and he dries off. Because he eats beer, sandwiches, leftovers on the day of r & r after skating Sunday and all week he is hungry for it and Sunday is a day for den, for sauna and rink and Mik says Sunday is my eating day and you gotta be hungry for it, says he.

Because Mik chose puck, Mik says this and says move yer feet while Mik keeps his own dead still skates swole and crossed.

Because Mik would rather since.

Because since Mik lost, he wears skates outside on the sidewalks.

Because Mik knew ice like his own palm, walking around on sidewalks did not feel right to him loafered.

Because Mik still had skates, still had spoils.

Because Mik did not still have his blondes.

Because it had happened to him.

Because Mik had had wives.

Because luck gets trapped in, you can't fuck with a good streak or bad streaks will come, says Mik.

Because sons have to do with luck, girls have to do with luck, has to do with numbers and stats.

Because Mik's no good at math, luck fucked him.

Because Mik wobbled, took a loss and lost all of what he thought he had. Because what he thought what he had was a marriage, a Missus Mik. Because what he had was a baby that he could not coach. Because he could not call his baby Mik, like his brother Mik or his brother Mik or his brother Mik or his cousins Mik and Mik, his uncle Mik, or his dad. Because his baby was not a Mik.

Because Mik did not have a son and did not want the girl.

Because sons and girls have to do with luck.

Because Mik had all the worst luck and Mik wanted what Mik wanted, the puck and the spoils, wives, trophies and sons.

Because Mik said son and meant Mik.

Because somewhere Mik means hockey.

Because Mik chose the puck, chose stick. Because his favorite color was black since grade one, since grade one he was what he was and he was both captain and coach and son I am not.

Oh, sore, am I ever?

Oh, I am sore.

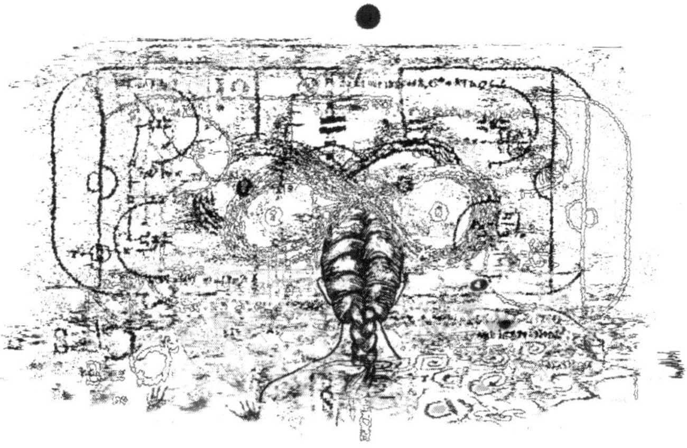

Mummies, Next, Mortar

Wet TP is like whisper, gets what song ears never hear even when listened to as careful as any girl could. The only lotion I have got is calamine. The only shampoo kills lice, scalps the skull with its ingredients, killing off the bugs that used to live in our hair. We would as kids pick at each other's little lices like tiny apes even after we had ran out of mayonnaise. We wet our sheets and we set the lice on fire. We wet the dog and they put her in the oven.

This cupboard is bare all besides. I am glued to the tube, hungry for hot wings and bleu, a wedge for the swelling. I am a nibbler. I tug at meat with careful bites. My index is sticky. Sweat dricks down.

I am just dirty.

I kissed a flying fuck on the mouth midair just before it went splat six feet deep, under the drink, beside the bones of my dust dog, Lo. Lo who died because her heart was her liver and her liver was a bone she swallowed whole. She swallowed a whole rope and that was what made her feel on fire and that was that.

But I can't be yours, I told him to myself. I can't be your sleeping dog. I can't wait these dog days whole. Could you be pleased to answer my questions?

His tongue is soap and watery and as slippery and I keep drinking. I drink how if I do, the bad taste will turn into the shiny and silver poisons that fall out of my mouth rotting the table and tasting how chewing dark grounds and wet bark would. So I, instead, swallow it all. If I swallow all of who I say, it does not spill out wet. All of who I say does not mess my chin, my neck, and make spill down. It is not soapy or runny.

Would it feel how it feels to swallow a whole rack of ribs whole and swallow way down the blood and the bite? I ask and I ask.

Calm down, Miss. An eel is an eel.

And as slippery as anyone.

I sucked on the eel so my head could rest peaceful Daylight savings six feet deep, under the drink, beside the bones of my Lo. How soft went that limp city! I found the chests were each empty when I pried. The more that I pried, the more I was slipped splinters. I have bought a lot of tweezers.

I say to him please.

I say, Say it please once out loud. Say, do you know what leapt? Do you know what went when you left?

Says he can't see me, but he sure can smell, and I taste how a girl tastes, how a land line stays put, still. Says he can't hear what I got to say, but he sure can smell, and I smell how a spoon shines in soapy water.

Waiting will kill a person how ropes do.

I keep to myself lying in the grass outside and waiting for him dungareed and calm how radiators stay in labor. I am outside the reunion. I am waiting for him to stop being fifteen, sixteen. I wait until the wet wedge on his plate stops tasting of a tongue and falls onto the floor so I can kiss it on its lips who knew him inside and out because he licked them like he was hungrier. He licked them like he could stand to gnaw. I wait and spin a radio fuzzy up. I wait how it is left out on the counter with all the lights on and the windows flung wide open, breezing threes.

Why are you an unopened man? I practice singing this out loud waiting outside for him in the grass. Ask him to grow his hair back overnight. Ask him to rip all the warts on him off and stop growing plaque this instant. It is that easy, I say.

He tells me whoa calm down like I could buck him off of me or neigh or whinny.

I am waiting for the grass to itch pink again, for calamine to verde verbatim.

Someday, he will say it but I will know those notes already. I will laugh in his face to keep from crying how a horse would cry, lips smacking, like he is some ring on fire that horse—must gallop up to unscared. Someday, I will rub myself raw, pink, and laugh. I will laugh my belly soapy, laugh until the belly waters silvering, falling out, keeping me from kissing. I chewed at my lips and they are both pretty puffy, but I still swallow them wholly, flying by the two-liter at a time, and still they taste to me of soapy water.

Land Blood Bank

I was going to tell you that I loved you and inform you of the wedding that had taken place in your sleep. Between whatever you wanted to wear, something you would wear to work, whatever you wanted because I want you comfortable, or maybe this costume change, maybe what you are to be donning are sweats. I know about you from what I have seen of you. In the glisten of valuable information overheard at blood banks, you chose to wear slacks climactically. That sludge out there. Sometimes I am vindictive, small, so as to be shapeless, puttering around the sidewalks, walking the same pattern, the same of the same. The plan was to take as many supplements as you are old and lie for you to discover your donor. You stomach-pump the bride. When they realize the value of these nutrients, they will insist on extracting them. I have not slept since the first day I read your name, decided to take it for mine. I have not slept one iota since so. The tape on the bag says we're wed. The mailperson asked when approaching the iron creak of the opening why? This is the echo you don't correct. I was to make a donation.

Under Doors of Foreigners

What I don't know about a house is which dream I will have sleeping inside of its strange beds, above its pallets when I am guest again.

I know that my mother made French fries for father at four a.m. in her mother's house, and it made her mother's house burn down. She fell asleep and the grease burned up even the family photos.

I know there are houses I have slept in where I've been bitten by spiders for closing my eyes. People eat spiders in their sleep every year they say. I think that's why I am always sleepy but never can. I also think a house can have a room that is so much of one person that you know them now so much you will finally sleep after all. Sometimes somebody wants you to be the room they fall asleep in so much that you never will.

I slept in a foreigner bed once, a mother and father's. They had two huge crosses above their headboard. I had a new tattoo. Their son laughed at my arm during dinner but covered his mouth. I didn't give more than one word before bed. Above where he slept, he had pictures of pigtailed girls and, too, of cartoons. I didn't understand the soap there, but I wanted to wash around where I started to sweat. I was scared about the ink, and there were so many bloody statues that I stayed awake feeling their marriage all over me.

There were gold-framed photos of their loved ones on either side protecting them. I wrapped my arm in a scarf and watched until the son woke up.

Turmeric

I met a man at a barbeque with no sense of smell. We talked about how neither of us could. It tasted rank in my mouth when he got done. Every time like mustard and onion.

He told my name to me when we did it. He dosed holding my hand. Then, the room sighed blue. I swatted under the bed for my license.

I popped zits on his shoulders, tried to read his tattoos. They were in cursive or some language. The pus sat in beads, splurred my thumbs.

I haven't turned thirty, I said.

What he told me was, Good.

What kind of man falls asleep before you? I've never been with a man who reeks of me. I cook since I get nervous. The man I cheat gives me stomachaches. He shouldn't have let me know he likes the way I smell.

My mom has a friend who's psychic. She finds lost kids. On dates, men take her to the theater. She was tiny like a child. I swear I've seen coats topple her over. They couldn't stay hooked.

I always hoped I could bring someone down.

Siblant Bling

Imbiber

An imbiber and I live together atop luscious grass in a blighty city. We pass for twins.

I have got no sense for this locale. We live near a casino, where I've never been. Could I hold a gambler in my hand? I like to feel I'm owed.

We try singing in unison to Canadian radio, but he fumbles Franco las. This rag we hang from the refrigerator is what I'm supposed to mind, but I keep letting it go. All these rules to our lives inside.

Look, it has grown young.

Spores, he says, which is something I would never say.

Is his penis as vibrant as his silver-tongued responses? thought I.

Unpromisingly squamous?

The kitchen is what I'm smitten with. It is cleanly fickly thanks to me. Our living room does well for itself. Its demeanor comes across better than the dividends. The chrysanthemums have gone and bummed me out.

I have abilities in the privacy of our home that I don't care to pass along. I get a lot done no one sees. I have grown to love a god, I think, though that's not a thing in vogue. A god made us make up clichés, so it seems there keeps on being wind forever.

The imbiber says people know me to me, and he feels it feels swell.

People whom?

A hullish win-win sinks in.

At night, I have come to find him nice, what with his robe. It is all about composure. He bathes in a hidden, masculine fragrance behind our scumming soaps.

He tells me things like, Geez, in the bathroom when I laugh at him. Lists of local businesses tarry his visits. I imagine legume crullers we could give for party favors. Our walls' purposes he named with an on-loan label gun. The coat I wear around is of raw hide.

I enjoy his vagina.

What Night Is

Threes.

We squeeze threes. We squeeze threes and One means one thing. Two means two. Three is this, is our singsong, when we walk, together or otherwise, around, locked. Our fingers make spiders. We give them voices. Nobody gets it but us.

We hold our hands opposite ways to explain. I hold mine straight on my heart when I say, It's like this.

Wake! Wake like emergency. Reach for a different-sized hand. Squeeze threes. Fall back asleep.

Twos.

When we sit in two chairs, we touch feet first to talk. It gets late in the cellar when we hide from the storms. Or maybe it is early, and it just seems late because it is dark, but at bedtime it is hands again telling stories through the number of squeezes. Only we can taste what the walls have to say. We report to each other through grips until the other one falls asleep.

We got another trick up our sleeve. We never had birthdays before. Four hands to spell out all of the digits we need until twenty. And then toes til we're forty.

The kids at the schoolhouse bring in sweets for their birthday. On my birthday, on Others', we walk to school like a regular day. Do the steps of the feet of the birthday kids bounce higher? Does the rubber lift them up into the air and make their insides skip?

We ask her, Can we buy crowns? Who she is, is Grammy.

What for?

Other looks at me, I look at Other. We know she means no.

Birthdays, Grammy says, are pagan. Jehovah, she says, does not like them. They are not nice.

We squeeze.

When we ask too much for something, all we see is cellar, and the cellar is too dark to see. I—with us, feel our way down the steps. Down the steps, we each take a wall side by side. Other, he's left and me, I am right. These walls are made out of not real wood. We licked this wood once and it tasted brown.

Lick this wall with us.

You're making that face. It tastes bad.

Do what I do.

He sticks out his tongue and rubs it against the muck brown wall. See the starlight and the roadlight from the headlights passing by the high baby window. The big window upstairs is high baby's Grammy.

Up we walk, sit on the couch. The vacuum eats muck out of the carpet. It is that hungry. It sounds mad. It has frown in its sound, and I see the sound face of its humsong. I am afraid and reach for a different sized hand.

Lift up your feet! Other says to me.

We grip and grasp and lift up our socked feet. When we lift up our socks, we lift them as high as the other one's sole. We have the same legs so long as we raise them the same highness.

You might be catching up, says Grammy. You'll start to get growing pains.

She is watching us lift, matching our feet.

I don't say anything, listen to her speaking English to me in specific.

You know that you grow in your sleep, says Grammy. You're growing all the time. Did I say that to you ever?

Then, I knew what was night. Night was what made Other big and what made me small. Night is what made us two not the same. I will tell you a secret. I will whisper it with my tongue to your ear, but not in spider. After that, when I say I slept good, I hot lava lie.

We got to make crowns, I say.

We never had a birthday before. We did not know what one looked like, and so we draw it. We don't ask Grammy. That would not be nice. I look over at what he draws, and what he draws is this: a brown cake, purple teeth, yellow for the sun. Our birthday, we make up. It comes when warm meets cold and holds its hand. Some call this tornado weather. Some say, Time to go down into the cellar.

This night, I'm awake not doing the growing. Other grows more and grows more in his sleep. I hear sirens that whine vacuum loud. They make shapes on the gray walls, red and blue.

Time to make plans.

Grammy won't like it. And Jehovah won't like it, he says.

I tell him in spider to stop. Here we go turning older. We got to have a birthday.

Other goes to sleep that night, and I ask Jehovah, did you hear what I said?

I lay out our clothes right next to each other on our bed. The clothes look like us lying down with no heads at night.

That morning, Other says, Did you sleep good?

I sleep. Find me scissors. Cut out shapes. Trace our shapes and cut them, I say.

When he traces, I get the scissors and make scissorsnips on a green apple. The apple is green and yellow at the same time. We both got a brown spot on our ring finger. I cut it off on purpose. I slice the spot open. Blood pours on my apple. Other puts down his fat marker.

Your apple is rusting, Other says to me. You're making it dirty. Your spot's gone, what for?

It's my blood. I don't mind it.

He takes my thumbnail between his two fingertips. Runs them along the edges that are flaky. My blood gets on his hand, but we let it dry. Then, he rubs it with his tongue until it disappears.

And after, we seek through the cellar. Foil is hiding and we are doing the seeking. We find foil. It is shinier than the stars that shine in the high window when it is night. He has not seen them, and I want to tell him.

We hold foil under this window between our indianstyle leg table making a sea. We move the metal blanket. The foil waves crinkle in our ears. They make our spines tickle, and our ears feel kisses. We ripple secrets that make the sea up.

The foil is silver and crunchy. Under our fingers, the foil is scratchy.

Put it in your mouth, I tell Other.

We want to taste silver how we hear it. When we lick with our tongue, it is ick.

I have not slept in twelve sleeps.

Grammy is starting to notice I think. She says You best sleep or you'll never catch up. He is growing bigger and bigger with each hour.

I think quick.

She goes out to the car and leaves to knock on doors with a lady who does not speak English.

Down the cellar, I go careful in socks. Stepping slow, licking the wall. It feels and tastes brown.

I say I dreamed he dreamed he was driving.

Remember when we drived?

Yeah. On the lap.

By Loren Grove?

On ice.

Where did you go? The store?

No. To Kingdom Hall.

A hand reaches for hands and makes spiders, speaks spider. *Lumdumdum. Leetlelaylee.*

What did you dream?

I don't remember, ever.

I don't say what I dreamed. He knows what I do at night.

Other's eyes shut up. He is getting shuteye. He is breathing different, stretching. I look at him sleeping. Nighttime is time for nightmare.

Is Nightmare a horse? Two words put together, like cardboard or sandbox. We've been learning about them at the schoolhouse. We've been adding together tablecloth and moonbeam and sunshine and starlight and birthday.

Papercut and scissorsnip. Soupspoon and saladfork. Tongs sounds like tongues. We lick with them. Lick the walls. We've been learning how to set tables. We forget to fold up the napkins.

Do you think Nightmare is a horsey? What is night?

I don't know, I pretend. I don't want to ride her if she is it. A horse is a merry-go-round. There's a buckle, okay? I don't like the faces. The music neither.

I whisper this to him in spider, my fingers dancing over his belly.

The sun falls flat on her face. The sky is a lava lie. My tummy tumbles ooze and stings. When I took those scissors and cut off my spot, I took a secret picture in my head. That picture shines milken and silver. I like to look at it while he dreams, the cut-off spot.

It feels early, but we don't go to school. It looks like it is bed, but it is any o'clock. We just woke up. There's whispers between us. Hands join hands and make spiders. The spiders are sizzling secrets between wind. They climb high over wooden rectangles we sleep under. Rectangle because it is not equal sides.

What is night? Other asks in spider. I think he knows I am not sleeping. I give the dead fish to him pretending not to know. The dead fish means there is no knowing.

We are about to go sleep when Other says so.

If it storms, I don't want a birthday.

I pretend sleep.

The Ones Before Ones

Other sleeps sound. He never wakes up afraid. But I sometimes see him smiling, dog sleeping. Sometimes see him kicking, dog dreaming. Sometimes feel the fearings. When he reaches for me, he lets out some web.

I see myself wide awake. If I sleep I dream myself stretching so long I'll outgrow the other, and he will be little. We are splitting to ones from awe in this dream. This is a taste just like wall, like foil. This is a scissorsnip sting.

That night my legs do not stretch to meet Others. Growing pains, Grammy calls them. She moves slow when there are storms. I been watching her close. I squeeze Other in one twos.

You go down there, she says. I need a rest. A storm is in my bones. You two be safe and go down.

I can't tell time and don't ever want to know how.

We start to stack boxes like we been planning. We been making plans to climb those boxes. We pile them high to the window. I climb up, but Other won't come.

It's dark, Other says.

This is night. This is a storm.

This is not what a birthday is. I told you.

When his spider drew, it used green for trees. He used brown for cake, purple for teeth. It drew on boxes. The boxes tell stories some web spun.

It's not our birthday. We don't have one. You were one and I was two. I am littler. I tell him in spiderspeak, This outside? This is what night is.

His eyes fill with fear. You don't know night. You sleep.

I do so know, I tell him.

My belly feels ick like when we lick foil. My belly flops over, slips soapy. I lied with my tongue to his ears.

I put on my crown. The wind is yelling. Other's not coming. The wind tastes funny. It blows up my nose. It blows my hair up and steals my crown.

You get down from there!

I go up. I cannot watch him so scared of me.

Get back, says Other. He reaches, squeezes the air spinning a web to pull me back with him. I do not want him to see where the colors wind up.

Cover your eyes. This is night.

He hides. I fit through the baby window with scrapes and ripped open knees. The scar is lump after lump. The wind takes me sideways. The sound is a siren. I can't see him. I can't taste the walls. It was then that I could not find words, could not say them in spider.

Now I'll be alone in a storm in traffic. Ambulance sirens spin blue and red (in the dark (or by day in the rain). I get the worry inside of my gut. The missing or warnings. A feeling for left-down car windows. Or ovens. Chalk left outside, bleeding colors all over cement into sewer drains. Sometimes I squeeze the steering wheel once and twice and press in the clutch with my might, to send a message to wake up Other.

Later, I ask the sky, Did you hear what I said?

To drive the point home, my hand sits on my chest. I look up. I try with my might to heal whoever I heard fly by inside of that ambulance. Did you hear me?

Now, strange hands shake our hands. In this newness, we don't want to give the dead fish to them, but we do not want them to squeeze so hard it feels squeezed in its bones. It is electric: a sunburnt soreness. It is a sting when another presses your bones in while muttering your name, repeating it into your hand. When we got a secret, we squeeze all the knowledge inside of the other one so no one can hear.

After, I get a sick feeling remembering a sentence in spider. Hiding from the lightning of it, I guess. After storms, does the planet earth made of rock feel this way down there where lava is alive, all from the sky making wet? Does lava leave blind, deaf and dumb when it leaves for the surface to breathe real air? Between squeezes, there are secrets and hot lava lies. Those secrets are all that is mine.

Tapioca

The Finns were mostly our cousins, brown and blondes. They were They Who Play Rough. They would pry cinderblocks from the ice with shovels to chuck at us. They would light our dolls' hair on fire, and the smell was a smell like the smell of a burnt-up diaper.

The smallest of us wore them, sometimes, out.

We would get dropped off by Aippä. She would leave, it seemed, for forever. We passed the hours by the house of the neighborman who took stake in his mailbox. He buried, our cousin said, his brother under there.

The neighborman was from a town called what sounded like Tapioca. Our Finnish cousins down the road burned our hair, pulled up by the handful, held us swung by the fist. They hid our mittens, stiffed our fingers.

We hated tasting Tapioca how we hated the elderly canned tuna sandwiches. We spat the alfalfa over sinks. We hated afternoon date squares, their smells.

The Finns did not have to bathe. They washed up in their ukki's shack he made. They would put it against us: his own two hands. The shack was a test, a place you throw water on rocks and with your sounds long say sauna. You try to steam out the wuss, try to make them not breathe. You are something if you do not need to lift the ladle, get bucket water up to your nostrils to stop the singeing. Blow on your cousin's skin, he might yelp. You might sting him so he cannot breathe inside the shack.

The top shelf champ would keep you bowing on the low bench, if you braved staying. If you stayed, you would be breathing into your innie or outie, you would be folding. Bow down to the big boy or girl who would dunk your head in the bucket water and hold it fossilized for you. The wuss would gust out the door. They would run a cold path. Swim backwards and stare at the shack and pray. Backstroke all the way to Bootjack, to Dreamland where they sell tough steaks. You had to feed the fire as wuss. Open the iron box, black and wicked, scraping your spine, this noise, this croak worse than a frog fried against the grill of Aippä's car. You had to ball up old articles about your uncles and their sports. You crumbled the recruits and the strawberry festival queens and the burden on us because of the lost mine.

Our cousins were brothers and ugly. Their underwear was hanging on clotheslines in the front yard. They skipped school to make up games, to kill crawfish with their boots. Their long johns dangled with spew. Täti could not get to scrubbing their gunk. Our mother scrubbed blood out of her silken slips and underpant crotches, we had watched. Our mother often got called into the office.

Tapioca seems like spew seems and stays. The town is called another name. To us, it is still Tapioca, what we know of it: snowplows on Finlander roadnames, the neighborman, carhoods, pylons in the driveway, the occasional parade. The neighborman comes out, sits on the hood. He shakes open his newspaper, wears binoculars.

We like to be spied on. We hate neighbors. We hate Tapioca and pudding-type things tasting too vanilla.

It is because we play dead the neighborman goddamned us. We lie on his lawn, and one of us crosses our arms over the grave of his good-for-nothing brother. One of us plays pooch. The hamtongue of a dog, a cold cut pink to drip spit. We see *X*s for eyes, how our fingers nub crayons, pressing too hard drawing suppertime trout. At our cousins', we must eat dead trout straight from the bay, off wusses' wormed lures.

The neighborman has got no garage, no kids, no wife. He has ice cold beverages. We hear Would you care for a beverage when Täti brings in the relatives.

We get ourselves locked out of houses. We get fed roast under the clothesline. We hold down our cousins' brother and drown him pretend, hold down the one in diapers next. We play resurrection, make mummy bandages. We use this word we heard—appendages. The sissy one plays Mary Magdalene. It makes the day long. We feel like hamtongued dogs.

Nobody tucks us in tight. We wait for headlights to blind us through what is called a bay window. The one Finn we bring back to life. First, we kiss his nose and pen his palms. Then, we tickle his fist open when he won't go along and play dead how we would like. The sissy undresses the dead. The zippers sometimes catch. Dead Finn flinches when his skin is pinched up in his denim. We make fun.

Lie down, Sisyphus.

Reciting:

Bless us O Dog

Give us some snack

If you do not

Then, we pause.

There are not enough seatbelts in our car. The middle ones pinch the chub. The metal is freezing, even in summer. We slide the buckle to unbore ourselves on Tapioca roads. The drive takes us a while, and we talk to ourselves in low tones. We play private games when we drive.

Aippä says, Silently, Silently.

When we stay with our cousins, we sleep outside under the sky with the bugs beeping. They itch, and we rash. Come one bag to the next. The sissy sneaks in, scared of outdoor sounds.

Some nights, we sleep almost naked. It is too much to burrow in our coffining bags. Keeping still makes the glitter bugs blink more on and off for us.

We don't know when she'll come for us.

She is in the bathtub, unhappy. She is soaking.

Leave me be.

We'll see, she'll say if we ask.

We go.

Then, she hangs a bed sheet in the backyard that is soaked like somebody got killed. Maybe the neighborman's family.

Our bed is too small, so we sweat glue together. Spiders nip our wrists. We welt. She leaves bleach out on the counter we think is juice. Pink insulation swigs and pulls our wall. We try to get over the cold.

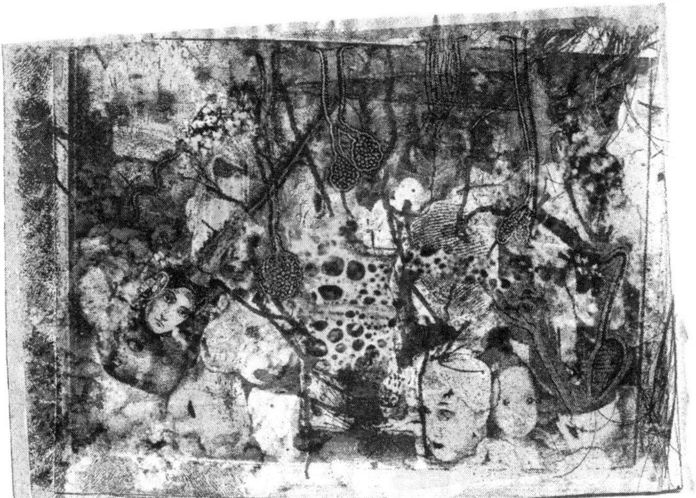

String Figures

We had it with Doll, her crying. Doll can't stop on the ottoman. She grips a bag of Globes. We are arraigned all evening. We're here with hope to sit, but she's hogged the whole sitting.

Our eyes fall up in our heads. We take turns—say, What is?

The face she makes looks like somebody, but nobody, died.

Dolly, Doll-Baby, we say, sugar-voiced and sisterly.

We would like to not squat. Lions do for queens.

If we ask her to move, will she spill?

Mussed, mussed.

When we ask, in our fists' reach, we steal some grapes. Our sister, the biggest, the oldest, won't stop honking.

Do I have to spell it out? She has the smock on again, our Doll. Her lashes drip octopus. The back cracker puts her back together.

We get string and start cup and saucers. The string is old from skates tied knotted.

Why aren't you out, Doll? We ask one at a time.

She doesn't speak. It'll take from us forever, making up things to say to her about her.

Our Doll, we can't touch. Her room has a roof and a chain and a lock. The door cracks on what she does.

The crying makes us wish for an arrangement.

Medora, No. Dakota

Doll-Baby won't do the dishes.

Blow.

I take it blonde.

Blow, it's hot.

Won't wash.

She is fetching, weighing wait, tapping toes, bent, sole to knee. All she has is her chook for the snow. All she has to get out is this—

Can't wash the hair?

Won't set then.

Never eats, like a swallow, but forever boils blanquillos, leaving shells on the table, fabled as a naysayer when it was required she dry.

Won't wash off.

There are wrecks, hills of crust. There are remnants, undiscovered meals, every sandwich ever sidewaysed, every knife ever glopped, gagged in fat-free.

The pans, the pans.

Meals are boiled alive, screeching or something. Or, it is myth.

So we say, Crustaceans.

All scraps yeasty, the wrecked settings.

We could break—

Bad habits. She held the plate up.

Figures.

Can't keep house.

You are done with the doing of the dishes.

Scream now the name Doll.* Stomp up pieces of road from dull rubber slobber, muck strolls—could we call them that? (Was not a stroll so much as a run. Was not a meander so much as a stuck sprint to unknown, to go on, to get.)

Doll. Doll. DOLL DOLLY!

Doll-Baby.

Who burnt this black?

No matter.

Who chose the pattern?

It bothers, Doll.

Was it Mother?

She tries the kind of sleep that is no more than the sealing of lids.

Yes, left messes.

How the bracelets read was how she called: Dolly, Do La, Bead. She wore chiming trinkets with charms, little heads silhouetted in high-octaves. Names were engraved with miniscule commemoratives. Doll was known for this windy shimmer. From the porch, you could hear her twinkling birch.

It was what she could not keep on. She had lost some.

Each rag left, pink packets halved, the garbage liners filled with the artifacts: tablatures, her wrappers.

Our crusts turned crouton sans her. The day-olds off shelves crumble. Her underthings are in our sinks. The trick for a leak is a word that began with Fels.

There, leave her, lying, still.

Fasting.

Go on, blow over.

---

*Say til it's dull.

The Kind There Are in Florida

An Old Boy

Inside that skuzz, a heavy-hipped figure, she sees an old boy.

Vavoom, says the old boy.

He watches her vacuum the crumbs that she slid off the table. The stubble did not catch the crackers she slathered in stink cheese the market sells cheaply the day after cheeses should go bad.

The old boys love crackers. They won't eat off of napkins.

Ch ehv ay raeey?

She hates how we sound it out, that we have to. She gets mad when we try it and waste it.

It is each afternoon that she slides the dress over her heavy hips, scoots open windows, lies down on the couch. We do not own a scale.

Do my back up, she tells us.

Vavoom.

Her face stays with rash from the stubble. The couch misses the cover, the burlap. Hear the phone ticklish? It bucks against the wallpaper. It buzzes.

You will hear it ringing, hear and hear next-door dogs, the thunder barking. Like us they hate the sound. This is how we are the next-door dogs.

Unzip it.

It smells old.

The dress falls off and we press our fingers to our eyelids not wanting to see, to our nostrils not wanting to suck up the smell.

Where he is, we do not know. Gone or else.

By the time she gets to the rotary, she misses it. By the time, the power zaps out, the phone settles, sleepy there itself.

Her feet wet from spat rain, cold and shrunk.

The chain doors swing open—a storm.

Calendars tell us, but we still do not know. We cannot read, cannot see it. The power went out.

For a while, she squints at the rows, the numbers, how the moon is filled in whole roll or crescent. Then, she turns from *marzo* to *abril*, scowls, drops the chain down inside her mouth. The taste makes her lose her lunch, tastes how spoons shine, and she is sick, not wanting to hold down the *chévere* and salt crackers.

I cannot bear another, she says.

We got nothing to say. Wordless for why it is dark outside early as now, we are whistling at how snug the dress fits from the couch with no cushions. Whistling how fireworks fall down in *julio*, how she is jello, falls out at the top.

The clocks read back black. They say nothing, the wall one ticked on clicks.

Blame the battery.

She gets down on her back in front of us and uses her hands under, beneath the dress. The nails scratch that rash.

When They Do

When they sit, they do so cross-legged how we play pit-a-pat. They sit across, head on, indian styled. Look straight in his eyes, over her shoulder.

She sees him just like this when they do so. When they do so, they are looking right at it.

They sometimes yell and scream:

Oh!

Sometimes, they do so louder than we wish. They do so forever it seems, and then, they stop all the sudden. The calendar marks when they did. We do not mean for you to listen for it. We remember when we cannot help but hear. There is a marker writ. Go see for yourself. That dress got rips. The zipper came loose when she wiggled out a foal, legs in t-straps.

It should get sewn shut.

If you fixed—

It wouldn't fit.

The dress is a size small on those heavy hips.

Vavoom.

He vamoosed. We do not know where he went.

She gives a helluva. Gets awful deep in there.

Got knots?

Yes, yes.

Where?

Higher.

Higher.

He leaves her again. We do not know where. He goes though.

That day he went, the sky went. On this kind of day, the rest until dark is a loss. All the tired eyes under store lights when cars stop cannot wait. They wait for: beds, dads, a wife, or a dog to lay down on.

She uses her hands under there on the couch with no cushions. She is looking for the quarters that had fell out.

We Ask Her Where He Went

Where has he been?

It is the kind of looking after, the kind we are doing where we have to watch her—in case. As long as we can, we are watching for when she changes out of that dress and never puts it back on, never yanks it hard over those hips again.

She slides off clothes, slides the screen closed shut.

Have you even heard a word?

While we pedal our bikes, we hear a few words about how someone saw his car get hit they thought, how he was here just for the night.

Or got gas.

Or called from the Dakotas.

The Kind There Are in Florida

They met, she and the old boy, and she did not say a word to us about it.

We did not hear a thing from her. They met when she was seeing another one. Then, she saw this old boy. Right away she changed her mind altogether. You could tell by the look on her face. She gave us a look.

Both that she saw were from Florida.

We did not want to have to call him our dad. We did not have a say.

She saw, when she came to the place of both boys, both had alligator heads set on the coffee table.

Is that something that happens in Florida?

We think so too cause of how she hovers all over our lunches and swallows them whole to check that the food is not poison.

The Blanket Show

What she does she calls the blanket show. She covers up my shoulders with covers. Those are the given stars alive with bugs. She hits her pinkie to me and shuts off my tongue. I do not tattle. So long as we are awake still, this is how we keep stuck, and we call it the blanket show. Up we go on watching, ever up there folding fingers on crumby, sunken bellies, the toes of us. I hide from her stiff cloth that molds over. To hear her socks skip whoopses over our floor takes a day. I move where she halts. I wait for her to come say "Out of space"—that's what she says to get me. There is us only, no spot for light. She says she sleeps, but I do not believe what she says. She climbs out the window, she says. Stomps on the roof I am told, but she tells me so. She goes where she goes. The roof I have not seen since June. And so it is, and she leaves me here. I wait to hear thumps and a cuss. She is a roof top girl, she says. I ask her what I wonder.

Outside Sunnyside

The guardians explain how she should come with. If she stayed awake, she could stay up with them and talk, if she could fake it with quinine and pretend not to not want to drink her drink.

The women there are spindly, thickly liquored. There is no one she would like to say things to. There are things she has to do: get home on the train to her place where the rain fell and wet her daybed's daisied throw, the place where the kid shits. She was recurring to the kitchen roaches. They are off-color from the sewer leaking through the loft, to the place where she never slept, never could bring herself to do much else.

Outside the rain, she has not shaved. She is no looker, but people look.

They say she should not go home. She redeems at the bar where they go. The rain pelts the window, somehow belongs to it.

If she leaves, she will walk the train. She will wait in the roar with the rashiest kind of man.

Shifts

In a cellar, I lived with a man who was humungous. He was a freak when he grew tall young, he said. His knees had bone chips in them. This is why he had a hobble. I had stayed very tiny, which he liked and had listed as his number one must-have in the ad about who he would like to move in.

The walls where we lived were stone. The first time I saw the cellar, I followed him scuffing. He prickled at the click of my shoe.

Pick up your feet.

I hate to make a person mad. I tugged them off and climbed on his bed. I stood on his mattress above bricks to see how fucked of a slant.

Our bed was Siamesed.

My size made the most room for the both of us. We shared covers, which sometimes I stole. He never got mad about that. We slept in shifts. The part where we would switch who slept, our lapse, was when we would lie down beside one another to sleep through the droughts of no dreams. I blew out the nightlight after I ate soup in bed, from cold cans. I liked to turn my back to him and feel him there. I liked him breathing in the dark closer by than when he went to his side.

He wanted to know if I was staying once I had been there for a while. Mostly, I said to him softly, That may be.

I would count tiles. Spiders chomped at our might. Choruses inside me shucked corn. Sheet stains stayed awake with us looking up.

I adored the encrusted forks—I'd have to clean up after the two of us, after we deserted our pannukakku.

They made it from the place I came from with a bay and a county song for when there was no snow. Where we lived, we would sing through the radio out an old call for the patron saint of precipitation. I found I never summoned her now. When the sky leaked through the cracks once in awhile in our home, I felt something like batter without the leavening.

Here is a secret: I do care for being bundled, which was the draw for me living underground, where it is meant to stay cold. I like kindling. I love to be spun.

In the kitchen in the dark before there is sun, it is me in the sink at the bakery where I make ends. The baker comes in after I slashed my batard. Our refrigerator hums low along to what we do like a little grandmother.

The sheets account for the way we sit still and fuss our lips over cups. When I piss, I flip the fan, so I consider the sinkspout without hearing his sneezing. Then, I try to remember my dreams when I open my eyes.

Once before sleep, he said a doctor called his heart too large as a boy. It seemed he had said I know how I need. He told me if I found him to not leave the sheets on our bed.

I could not imagine being responsible for digging open the earth.

Cardamom is the name of the spice in the bread I braid. I bake in the night for work. I bleach the spice out of my nylons on my breaks: the mildewed roux.

In life, I am the queen, yes, in charge of anything having to do with foods. I make us ham sandwiches, the lettuce limply bowed out.

I want to make myself up to the daylight somehow. The way I lived, there was our sleeping and yeasts from the breads.

There were not too many nights where I felt something final. I got frightened to think this would be the way. I thought about eating only onions I had grown down below, the occasional rutabaga. I thought, I am tired of candelabra.

His moustache fell into the sink one morning and, worried, I dabbed at the fixture once he left to clean homes. He asked me to bite him until the bruises left yellow highlighter where his arms felt numb.

I once saw someone take a nail to a person.

When he turned over in bed, I had private thoughts about a room.

It was, after all, an agreement, I said to him through space. I saw just his back, but his light was kept on long after dawn. I was afraid to turn it off.